Yo! Yes?

BY

Chris Raschka

SCHOLASTIC INC.

NEW YORK   TORONTO   LONDON   AUCKLAND   SYDNEY

ISBN 0-590-20557-9

Copyright © 1993 by Christopher Raschka.
All rights reserved.
Published by Scholastic Inc., 555 Broadway, New York, NY 10012, by
arrangement with Orchard Books.

12 11 10 9 8 7 6 5 4 3 2 1   4 5 6 7 8 9/9

Printed in the U.S.A.   14

First Scholastic printing, September 1994

FOR

my parents

Yo!

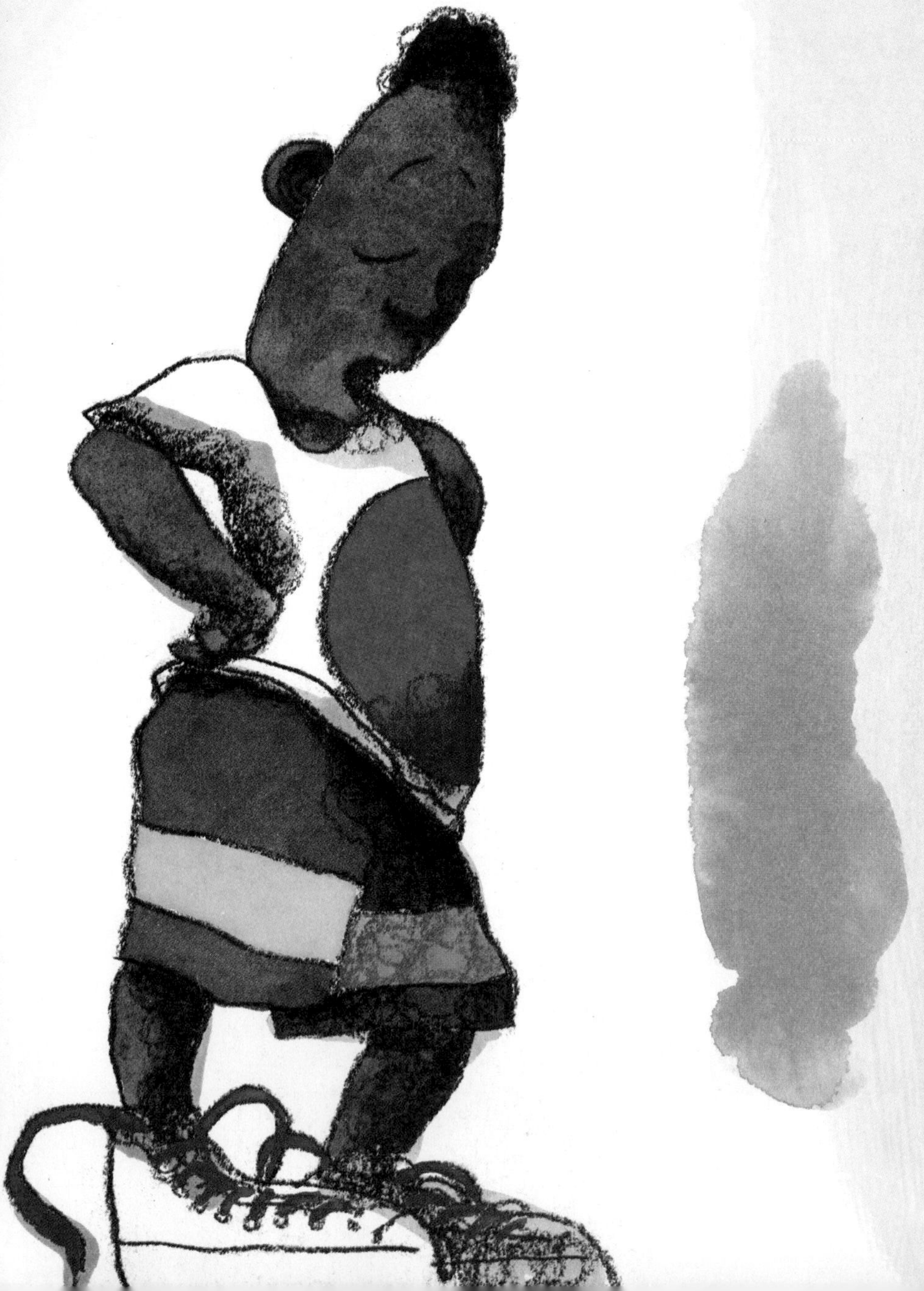

Yes?

Who?

You!

Me?

Yes, you.

Oh.

What's up?

Not much.

Why?

No fun.

Oh?

No
friends.

Oh!

Yes.

Look!

Hmmm?

Me!

You?

Yes, me!

Well?

Well.

Yes!

0-590-20557-9   Scholastic Inc.   RL1 004-007